BOOKS
GIVE US
WINGS
04-05
SCPL
St. Charles Public Library
Family Read-Aloud Book Club
Presented in honor of:
Alexander Pfaff

Bubble Trouble

First Aladdin edition January 2004

ALADDIN PAPERBACKS
An imprint of Simon & Schuster Children's Publishing Division
1230 Avenue of the Americas
New York, NY 10020

Book design by Debra Sfetsios
The text of this book was set in Century Schoolbook.

Printed in the United States of America
2 4 6 8 10 9 7 5 3

Library of Congress Catalog Card Number 2003106063

ISBN 0-689-85710-1 (Aladdin pbk.)
ISBN 0-689-85711-X (lib. bdg.)

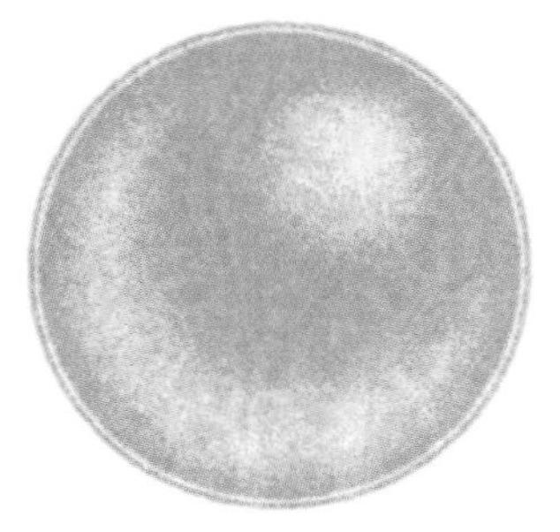

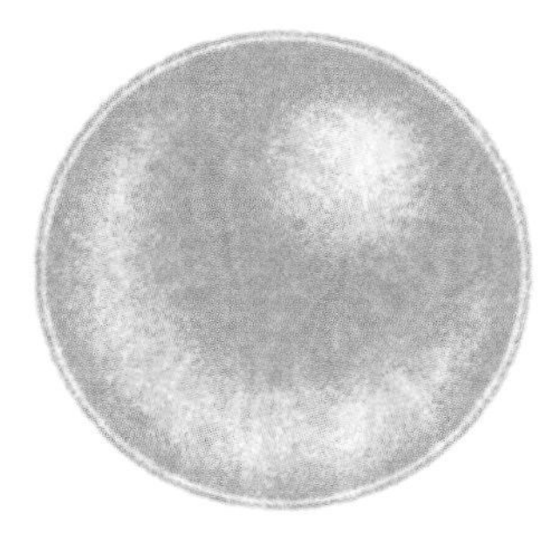

Bubble Trouble

by Stephen Krensky

illustrated by Jimmy Pickering

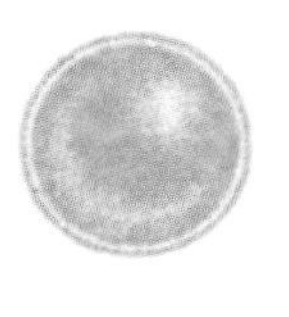

ALADDIN PAPERBACKS

New York London Toronto Sydney Singapore

One bubble.
No trouble.

Two new bubbles.
Three bubbles, four bubbles,
falling on the floor bubbles,

bouncing out the door bubbles.

Over books, under chairs,

bubbles spilling
down the stairs.
Through the hall,
on the wall.

Bubbles on
the grass outside.
Going, going,
overflowing.

Bubble shirts
and bubble pants
do a little
bubble dance.

Bubbles climbing up a tree.
Birds scatter, squirrels chatter.

Over cars, down the street,

bubbles bubble,
bubbles double.

Sweet bubbles on the rise,

Bank bubbles—
big surprise!

Bubbling boat,

bubbles float.

Will bubbles never stop?
Sun gets hotter.
Bubbles pop.

Bubbles bursting,

bubbles breaking,
bubbles busily unmaking.

Bubbles going—
three, two, one.

Bubbles gone. Bubbles done.

Make more bubbles?

Bubble fun.